It's Easy To Play Blues.

Wise Publications
London/New York/Sydney

Printed in England by
Caligraving Limited Thetford Norfolk

Farewell Blues

Words & Music by
Elmer Schoebel/Paul Marsh/
Leon Rappolo

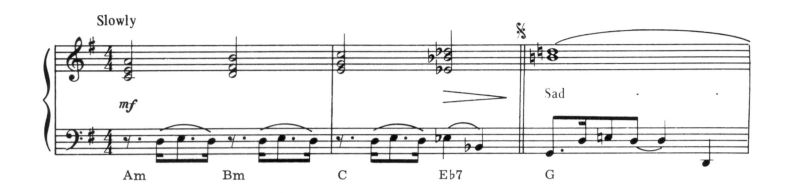

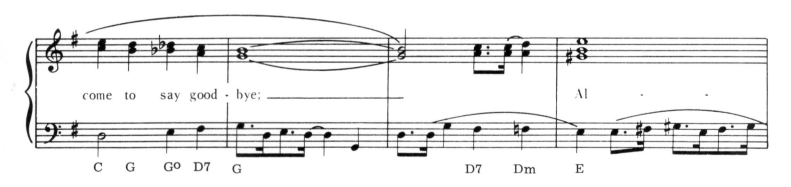

Honolulu Blues

Words by M.J. Gunsky
Music by Nat Goldstein

These Foolish Things

Words by Eric Maschwitz
Music by Jack Strachey

CHORUS

1. A ci-gar-ette that bears a lip-stick's traces
2. Gar-den-ia per-fume ling-'ring on a pil-low,
3. First daf-fo-dils and long ex-ci-ted ca-bles

An air-line tick-et to ro-
Wild strawb'ries on-ly sev-en
And can-dle-light on lit-tle

Eb   Cm   Fm7 Db Bb7   Eb   Cm
(Gsus)

-man-tic pla-ces
francs a ki-lo
cor-ner tab-les

And still my heart has wings,___ These foolish things remind me of

F9   Bb13 Bb7+ Eb9   Eb7 Eb7+ Ab   C7   F9

you.

A tink-ling pia-no in the next a-part-ment,
The park at eve-ning when the bell has sounded,
The smile of Gar-bo and the scent of ros-es,

Ab6   Bb7   Eb   Cm   Fm7 Db Bb7
(Gsus)

Those stumbling words that told you
The 'Ile de France' with all the
The wai-ters whist-ling as the

what my heart meant;
gulls a-round it,___
last bar clo-ses,___

A fair-ground's painted swings,
The beau-ty that it springs!
The song that Cros-by sings,

Eb   Cm   F9   Bb13 Bb7+   Eb9   Eb7 Eb7+ Ab

These foolish things re-mind me of you.

You came, you saw,
I know that this
How strange, how sweet

C7   F9   Bb7   Eb Ebo Eb7   Ab   Ab6

10

you con - quered me. _____ When you did that to me I
was bound to be. _____ These things have haunt - ed me, for
to find you still. _____ These things are dear to me for that

Abm   Db13   Db9   Eb   Gb9

some - how knew that this had to be. The winds of March that make my
you've en - tire - ly en - chant - ed me. *mp* The sigh of mid - night trains in
seem to bring you so near to me, The scent of smould 'ring leaves, the

B7   Bb7   Eb   Cm

he art a dan - cer, A tel - e phone that rings, but
emp - ty sta - tions, Silk stock - ings thrown a - side, dance
wail of steam - ers, Two lov - ers on the street who

Fm7   Db   Bb7   Eb   Cm
(Gsus)

who's to an - swer? ___ Oh! how the ghost of you clings! These fool - ish
in - vi - ta - tions. ___
walk like dreamers. ___

F9   Bb13 Bb7+   Eb9   Eb13 Eb7+ Eb7   Abmaj7   F7

things _____ re - mind me of |1. you. . |2. you.

Eb6   Bb7+   Eb   Abmaj7 Bb7   Eb

11

A Blues Serenade

Words by Mitchell Parish
Music by Frank Signorelli

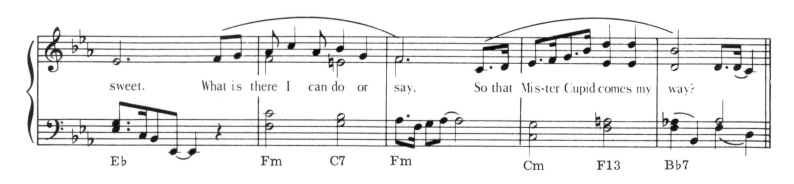

CHORUS

Moonglow

Words & Music by
Will Hudson/Irving Mills &
Eddie De Lange

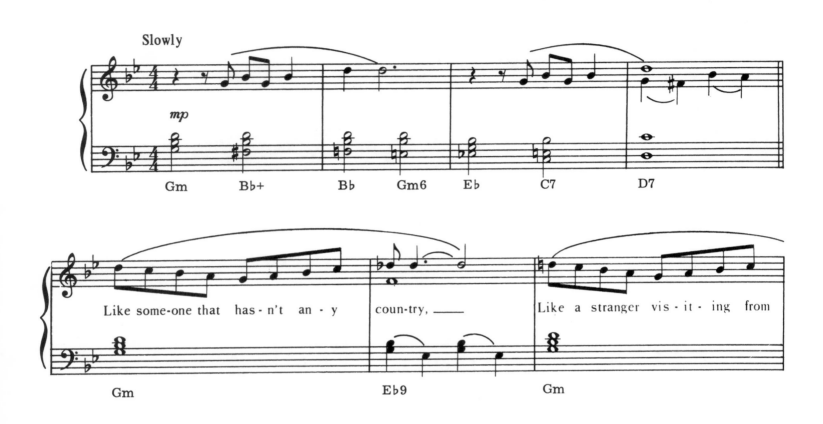

CHORUS

It must have been Moon - glow,   Way up in the
Am7   Cm (Bsus)   G6

blue,   It must have been Moon - glow
A9   Am7   D13

that led me straight to you.___   I still hear you
G6   Eb7   Cm6 Eb7 G6   Am7

say - ing,   'Dear me, hold me fast.''   And I start in
Cm (Bsus)   G6   A9   Am7

pray - ing,   ''Oh Lord, please let this last.''   We _____
D13   G6   Eb7   Cm6 Eb7 G6   G9

Stormy Weather

Words by Ted Koehler
Music by Harold Arlen

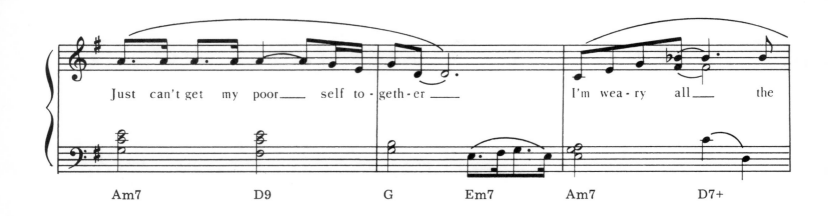

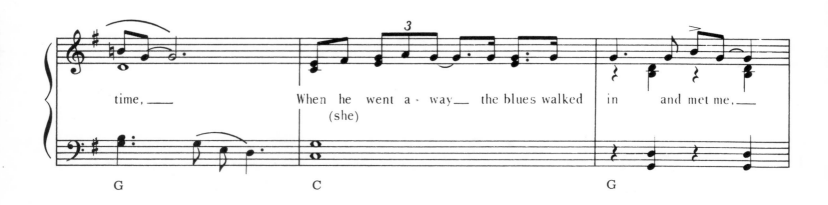

Moanin'

Words by Jon Hendricks
Music by Bobby Timmons

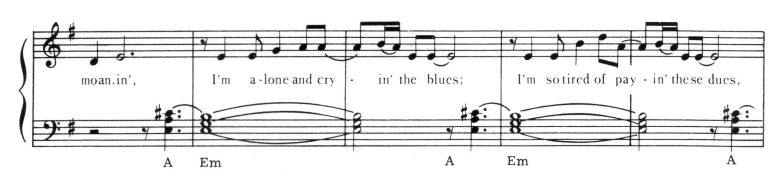

In A Sentimental Mood

Words & Music by
Duke Ellington/Irving Mills &
Manny Kurtz

The Creole Love Call

By Duke Ellington

Mood Indigo

Words & Music by
Duke Ellington/Irving Mills/
Albany Bigard

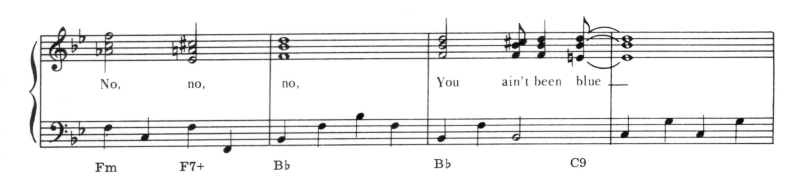

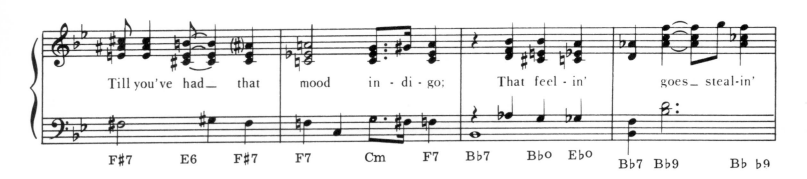

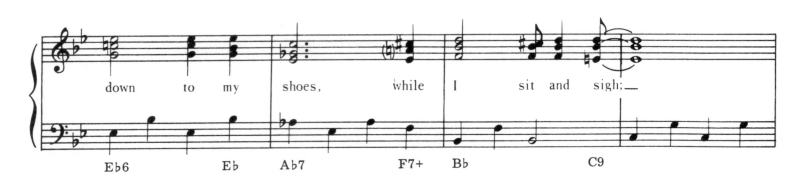

When It's Sleepy Time Down South

Words & Music by
Leon & Otis Rene/Clarence Muse

Basin Street Blues

Words & Music by Spencer Williams

Yes, sir - ee,___ where wel-come's free,___ Dear to me, where can I lose,___

My Bas-in Street Blues.

Fine INTERLUDE

Repeat Chorus

Solitude

Words by Eddie De Lange/
Irving Mills
Music by Duke Ellington

Sophisticated Lady

Words by Irving Mills &
Mitchell Parish
Music by Duke Ellington

Stardust

Words by Mitchell Parish
Music by Hoagy Carmichael

Another Shade Of Blue

Traditional

The Cotton Mill Blues

Traditional

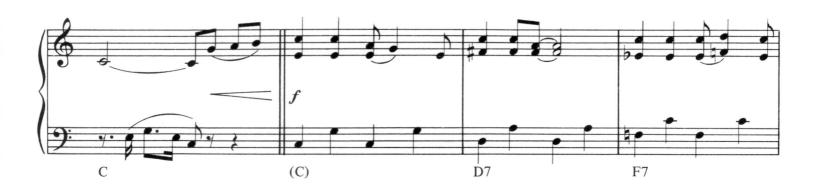

45

Worried Man Blues

Traditional

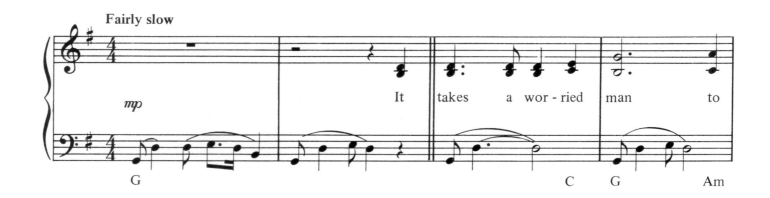

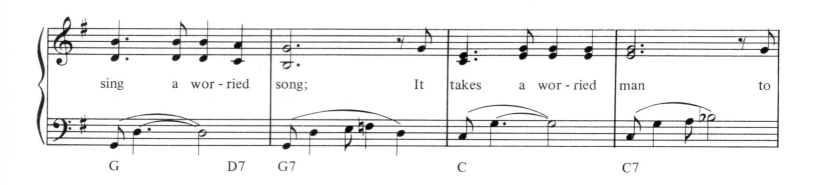

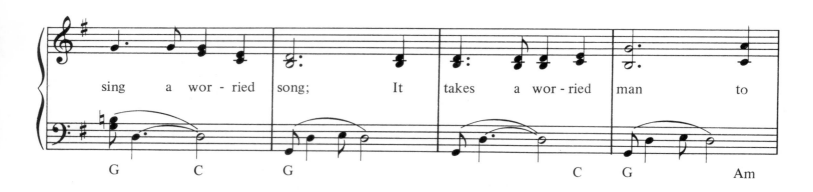

47

11/95 (22857)